Reading
BOROUGH COUNCIL

Reading Borough Libraries

Email: info@readinglibraries.org.uk

Palmer Park 0118 9015950
Southcote 0118 9015109
Tilehurst 0118 9015112

KT-168-683

Who Ate Auntie Iris?

Reading Borough Council
34126003506253

To Sebastião – ST
To Isaac – HS

Who Ate Auntie Iris? © Frances Lincoln Limited 2012
Text © Sean Taylor 2009
Illustrations © Hannah Shaw 2012

The moral rights of Sean Taylor and Hannah Shaw have been asserted

First published in Great Britain and in the USA in 2012
This early reader edition published in Great Britain in 2013 by
Frances Lincoln Children's Books,
74-77 White Lion Street, London, N1 9PF
www.franceslincoln.com

All rights reserved

ISBN 978-1-84780-478-5

Printed in China

1 3 5 7 9 8 6 4 2

Created in consultation with language and literacy
development specialist, Prue Goodwin.

Who Ate Auntie Iris?

READING
BOROUGH COUNCIL
3412600350625
PETERS 29-Oct-2013
CER4

By
SEAN TAYLOR
illustrated by
HANNAH SHAW

FRANCES LINCOLN
CHILDREN'S BOOKS

Look where Auntie Iris lives.
She's my favourite aunt. And sometimes my mum brings me over to spend the afternoon with her.
But Mum says, "My nose twitches every time I get here. And when a chinchilla's nose twitches it means there's danger in the air!"

Auntie Iris just smiles and tells us,
"There's no need at all to worry!"
But she does climb up the stairs in quite a bit of a hurry.

After all, on the first floor there's a family of bears.

And every time we go past their flat they give us hard bear stares!

On the second floor, there's this crocodile.

And I think there's something a bit too friendly about his toothy smile.

Then on the third floor, there's
a whole lot of wolves.

And every time they look at us
one of them always drools!

Luckily no one at all lives on the fourth floor.
So it feels safe from there up to Auntie Iris's door.
Or at least it did . . .

. . . until last Thursday afternoon.
Because Auntie Iris went down to put the rubbish out,
and she didn't come back!

I looked outside.
All I saw was her hat!
I crept down the stairs . . .

Not a sign of her!
And it seemed pretty definite to me that someone had eaten Auntie Iris!

I had to find out who'd done it. So I went to the first floor. And, although my nose was twitching with worry, I gave a tap on the door.
Next thing it opened wide, and a bear looked out.
I said to him, "Who ate Auntie Iris?"

The bear gave a scratch of his snout.
"It wasn't us," he replied.
"We're all sitting watching TV.
It's our favourite cookery programme today.
We watch it every week."

He seemed to be telling the truth. So I went to the second floor. I didn't like the thought of those teeth, but I gave a knock on the door.

Next thing it opened up and there was the crocodile. I said to him, "Who ate Auntie Iris?"

He gave me a friendly smile.
"It wasn't me," he replied, "and I'm sorry, you'll have to excuse me. Some friends have come round to help me install a brand-new jacuzzi."

He seemed to be telling the truth. So I went to the third floor. I knew that it must have been those wolves, and I banged quite hard on their door. One of them opened it up, but only a little bit. I asked him, "Who ate Auntie Iris?"

The wolf gave his lips a lick.
He said, "Who ate your auntie? Not us! We hardly know her! We're all of us having a quiet time in, and practising some yoga."

He seemed to be telling the truth too. So what was I meant to do? And who ate Auntie Iris?

I carried on up the stairs, thinking,

Was it the wolves? Was it the crocodile?

Was it the bears?

But then I heard a voice.
It said, "Ah! So there's my hat!"

It was Auntie Iris. She was all right!
"I thought someone had eaten you!" I said.
"Oh no!" she smiled back. "I just bumped into my new neighbours, and they showed me around their flat."

She led me back up the stairs.
I asked, "Are the new neighbours OK?"
Auntie Iris said, "They're lions!"

I turned round. They were looking our way.

"Chinchillas for neighbours!" said a lion.
"I can't say how happy we feel!
We'd very much like to ask you round,
and have you all for a meal!"

Auntie Iris just smiled and told me,
"There's no need at all to worry!"
But she did climb up the stairs in quite
a bit of a hurry.

More great TIME TO READ books to collect:

978-1-84780-476-1

978-1-84780-475-4

978-1-84780-477-8

978-1-84780-478-5

Frances Lincoln titles are available from all good bookshops.
You can also buy books and find out more about your favourite titles, authors and illustrators on our website: www.franceslincoln.com